Care♥Bears

Grumpy Bear™

and the GRUMBLE STORM

h

Hodder
Children's
Books

We are the

Care♥Bears™

Come and join us in Care-a-Lot...

I'm **Cheer.** I always look on the bright side!

I'm **Wonderheart.** I'm small, sweet and very curious.

I'm **Grumpy.** Inside, I'm really a big softie!

I'm **Tenderheart.** My heart is in the right place.

I'm **Harmony.** I know that music brings us together.

I'm **Share.** I'm happiest when I'm giving.

I'm **Funshine.** For me, every day's a fun day.

Grumpy Bear is feeling
happy. His favourite team,
the Care-a-Lot Captors,
are playing honeyball today.

Grumpy gets comfy in
his chair. He can't wait to
watch the match on TV!

"Hey Grumps! Let's watch together!"
Funshine arrives and starts nibbling Grumpy's snacks.

Harmony joins them.
"Honeyball!" she sings. "My favourite game of a-a-all!"
A little storm cloud puffs out of Grumpy's belly badge.

"Can I watch the match, too?"
asks Share Bear.

"Hello!" cries Wonderheart.
"Will you listen to my new song?"

"Not right now," replies
Grumpy, leaning closer
to the TV, while everyone
chatters around him.

"H-O-N-E-Y. HONEYBALL!"
Cheer Bear starts to dance
directly in front of Grumpy.

"This is the most important
part," grumbles Grumpy.

PEEEP!

The last whistle blows. The
match is over.

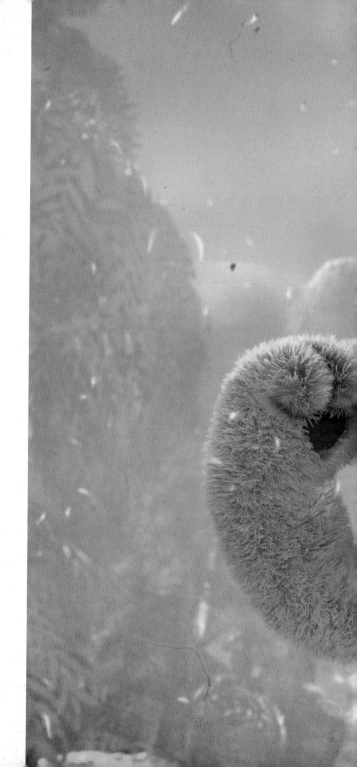

Poor Grumpy. He has missed the whole match.

The storm cloud over his head grows bigger and **bigger** and **bigger**. The sky gets dark and strong winds blow across the Moody Mountains.

Grumpy is making a grumble storm!

All the colours have been sucked out of Care-a-Lot!

Grumpy goes to find his friends.
He sees Harmony by the river.

"Leave me alone!" she shouts.

Grumpy scratches his head. He has never
seen Harmony cross before.

Next he spots Cheer.

"Ugly flowers!" she yells, throwing them down.
Grumpy looks at his friend completely shocked.

Tenderheart appears. He is floating in a big bubble!

"What are you doing in there?" Grumpy asks.

"This bubble is protecting me from your grumble storm,"
says Tenderheart.

Grumpy really wants to fix things ... but he doesn't know what to do.

Just then, Grumpy spots his friend, Funshine. All of his lovely yellow fur has faded.

"That's it!" decides Grumpy. "It's time to put things right."
Grumpy tells Funshine his best joke.

Funshine begins to laugh and – POP! – his colour returns.

"I feel like myself again!" he smiles.

Grumpy finds Harmony.

He cheers her up with a
relaxing paw massage. POP!
Her colour returns, too.

Grumpy calls Share and
Wonderheart over.
He gives them a
delicious cake.

"I feel so much better now,"
smiles Share.

Only Wonderheart stays
quiet. She is still in a
grump. Oh dear!

Grumpy thinks hard. There's
only one thing to do...

...Wonderheart needs a
Care Hug!

Wonderheart's
pretty pink colour
rushes back!

"I'm sorry that I caused a
storm," says Grumpy.

"Does this mean you won't
be grumpy ever again?"
Wonderheart asks.

"I'm not sure," chuckles
Grumpy. "I am called
Grumpy Bear after all."

HODDER CHILDREN'S BOOKS

First published in Great Britain in 2017
by Hodder and Stoughton

© American Greetings, 2017

american greetings

A CIP catalogue record of this book
is available from the British Library.

ISBN 978 1 444 93779 4

10 9 8 7 6 5 4 3 2 1
Printed and bound in China

MIX
Paper from
responsible sources
FSC® C104740

Hodder Children's Books
An imprint of
Hachette Children's Group
Part of Hodder and Stoughton
Carmelite House
50 Victoria Embankment
London EC4Y 0DZ

An Hachette UK Company
www.hachette.co.uk

www.hachettechildrens.co.uk

www.carebears.co.uk